How Rude!

For my Nan and Grandad, who have always taught me to consider other people's feelings. – C.H.W.

Quarto is the authority on a wide range of topics.

Quarto educates, entertains and enriches the lives of
our readers—enthusiasts and lovers of hands-on living.

www.quartoknows.com

© 2018 Quarto Publishing plc

Text © Clare Helen Welsh

Illustrations © Olivier Tallec

Clare Helen Welsh has asserted her right to be identified as the author of this work.

Olivier Tallec has asserted his right to be identified as the illustrator of this work.

First published in paperback in 2020 by words & pictures,

an imprint of The Quarto Group.

The Old Brewery, 6 Blundell Street,

London N7 9BH, United Kingdom.

T (0)20 7700 6700 F (0)20 7700 8066

www.quartoknows.com

A catalogue record for this book is available from the British Library.

ISBN: 978 0 7112 5355 1

9 8 7 6 5 4 3 2 1

Manufactured in Guangdong, China CC032020

FSC
www.fsc.org

MIX
Paper from
responsible sources
FSC® C008047

Clare Helen Welsh • Olivier Tallec

HOW RUDE!

words & pictures

"Hello Duck. It's lovely to see you."

"OOH!"

How rude!

"A tea party! Cool!

Hang these up!"

How rude!

"Ah, comfy! I'll start with a... sandwich."

"Which one would you like?"

"I only eat banana with ketchup!"

"Ham... nope!"

"Cheese... ew!"

Cucumber... definitely not!"

"I suppose they're not THAT bad."

SCOFF! SCOFF! SCOFF!

How rude!

"You must be thirsty after ALL that.

Would you like a drink?"

"This looks good..."

GLUG! GLUG! GLUG!

How rude!

"Oh, tea! Fill it up!"

"Yuck!
You forgot the sugar!"

HOW RUUUUUDE!

"CAKE!"

"I'll cut you a piece."

"What is taking so long?"

CHOMP! CHOMP! CHOMP!

TAP! TAP! TAP!

"HURRY UP!"

"Mmmm... mit wos dewicious!"

How... rude!

"Oh dear."

"What have we done?"

"I'm sorry.
I was rude."

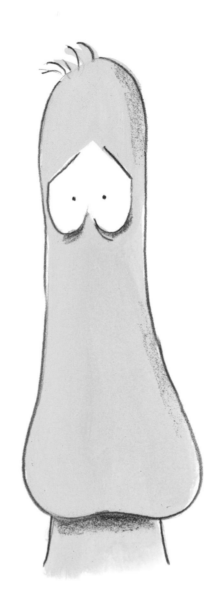

"I'm sorry, too."

"How delicious! Thank you."

"How polite!"